To Hilary Price,
who celebrates everyone

Text and illustrations copyright © 2011 by Mo Willems

Printed in Singapore
Reinforced binding

First Edition, October 2011
10 9 8 7 6
F850-6835-5-15089

Library of Congress Cataloging-in-Publication Data

Willems, Mo.
    Happy Pig Day! / by Mo Willems.—1st ed.
        p. cm.—(An Elephant & Piggie Book)
    Summary: Piggie celebrates her favorite day of the year, but Gerald the elephant is sad, thinking that he cannot join the fun.
    ISBN 978-1-4231-4342-0
    [1. Pigs—Fiction. 2. Elephants—Fiction. 3. Parties—Fiction.
4. Friendship—Fiction.]
    PZ7.W65535 Hap 2011
    [E]—dc22   2010034326

Visit www.hyperionbooksforchildren.com and www.pigeonpresents.com

By Mo Willems

Happy Pig Day!

An ELEPHANT & PIGGIE Book

Hyperion Books for Children/*New York*

AN IMPRINT OF DISNEY BOOK GROUP

Gerald!

2

3

Today is the
best day
of the
year!

6

10

It is the best day to have a pig party!

14

It is the best day
to play pig games!

It is the best day to say:

OINKY!
OINK!
OINK!

18

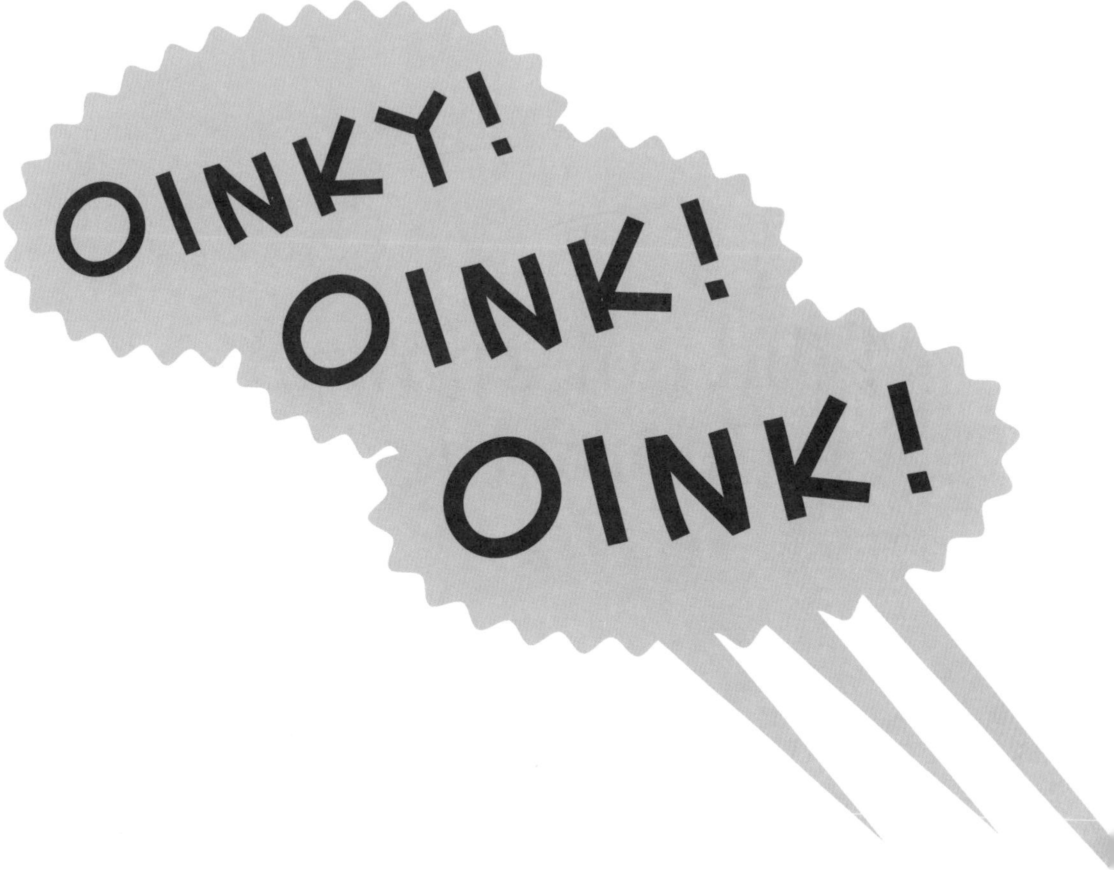

OINKY!
OINK!
OINK!

27

Isn't this
great, Gerald?

Gerald?

36

40

41

42

45

Happy Pig Day
is for . . .

51

Happy Pig Day to EVERYONE!

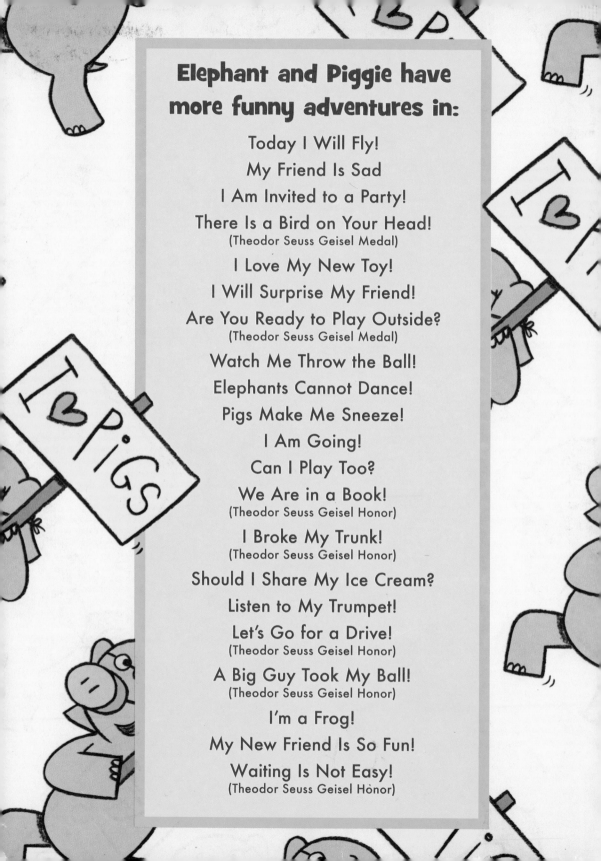

Elephant and Piggie have more funny adventures in:

Today I Will Fly!

My Friend Is Sad

I Am Invited to a Party!

There Is a Bird on Your Head!
(Theodor Seuss Geisel Medal)

I Love My New Toy!

I Will Surprise My Friend!

Are You Ready to Play Outside?
(Theodor Seuss Geisel Medal)

Watch Me Throw the Ball!

Elephants Cannot Dance!

Pigs Make Me Sneeze!

I Am Going!

Can I Play Too?

We Are in a Book!
(Theodor Seuss Geisel Honor)

I Broke My Trunk!
(Theodor Seuss Geisel Honor)

Should I Share My Ice Cream?

Listen to My Trumpet!

Let's Go for a Drive!
(Theodor Seuss Geisel Honor)

A Big Guy Took My Ball!
(Theodor Seuss Geisel Honor)

I'm a Frog!

My New Friend Is So Fun!

Waiting Is Not Easy!
(Theodor Seuss Geisel Honor)